Dear Parents:

Congratulations! Your child is taking the first steps on an exciting journey. The destination? Independent reading!

STEP INTO READING® will help your child get there. The program offers five steps to reading success. Each step includes fun stories and colorful art or photographs. In addition to original fiction and books with favorite characters, there are Step into Reading Non-Fiction Readers, Phonics Readers and Boxed Sets, Sticker Readers, and Comic Readers—a complete literacy program with something to interest every child.

Learning to Read, Step by Step!

Ready to Read Preschool–Kindergarten
• big type and easy words • rhyme and rhythm • picture clues
For children who know the alphabet and are eager to begin reading.

Reading with Help Preschool–Grade 1
• basic vocabulary • short sentences • simple stories
For children who recognize familiar words and sound out new words with help.

Reading on Your Own Grades 1–3
• engaging characters • easy-to-follow plots • popular topics
For children who are ready to read on their own.

Reading Paragraphs Grades 2–3
• challenging vocabulary • short paragraphs • exciting stories
For newly independent readers who read simple sentences with confidence.

Ready for Chapters Grades 2–4
• chapters • longer paragraphs • full-color art
For children who want to take the plunge into chapter books but still like colorful pictures.

STEP INTO READING® is designed to give every child a successful reading experience. The grade levels are only guides; children will progress through the steps at their own speed, developing confidence in their reading.

Remember, a lifetime love of reading starts with a single step!

Step into Reading, Random House, and the Random House colophon are registered trademarks of Penguin Random House LLC.

Visit us on the Web!
StepIntoReading.com
randomhousekids.com

Educators and librarians, for a variety of teaching tools, visit us at RHTeachersLibrarians.com

ISBN 978-0-7364-3594-9 (trade) — ISBN 978-0-7364-8181-6 (lib. bdg.)
ISBN 978-0-7364-3595-6 (ebook)

Printed in the United States of America   10 9 8 7 6 5 4 3 2 1

Disney
PRINCESS

Beauty and the Beast

by Melissa Lagonegro

illustrated by
the Disney Storybook Art Team

Random House 🏠 New York

Belle is kind
and smart.
She loves
to read.

Gaston wants
to marry Belle.
She does not
like him.

Belle's father, Maurice,
is an inventor.
He goes on a trip.

Maurice gets lost

in the forest.

Wolves surround him!

He finds a castle.

He goes inside.

Maurice meets
magical objects.
Lumiere is a candlestick.
Cogsworth is a clock.

The castle belongs
to the Beast.
He locks Maurice
in a cell.

Belle finds Maurice.
She asks the Beast
to free her father.

She tells the Beast
to keep her instead.
The Beast agrees.

Belle meets
the magical objects
in the castle.

Lumiere sings.

Belle explores
the castle.
She finds a magic rose.

The Beast finds Belle.

He grabs the rose.

Belle is scared!

Belle leaves the castle.

Wolves surround her.

She is in danger!

The Beast arrives.

He fights the wolves.

He saves Belle!

Belle returns

to the castle.

She and the Beast

become good friends.

They spend time outdoors.

Belle teaches the Beast
to dance.
They are happy.

Belle sees her father
in a magic mirror.
He looks sick.

Belle leaves
to help him.
The Beast is sad
when Belle leaves.

Gaston wants
to find the Beast.
He goes to the castle.
He attacks the Beast!

The Beast is hurt.

Belle is very sad.

"I love you,"
says Belle.

The Beast
is really a prince!
Belle's love changes him
into a human.
They live happily
ever after.